S0-AIE-537

Union Public Library
1980 Morris Avenue
Union, N.J. 07083

A SCIENCE

The Magic School Bus®
CHAPTER BOOK

The GIANT GERM

SCHOLASTIC INC.
New York   Toronto   London   Auckland   Sydney
Mexico City   New Delhi   Hong Kong   Buenos Aires

Written by Anne Capeci.

Illustrations by John Speirs.

Based on *The Magic School* Bus books
written by Joanna Cole and illustrated by Bruce Degen.

The author would like to thank John F. Farina
for his expert advice in preparing this manuscript.

If you purchased this book without a cover, you should be aware that this book is stolen property. It was reported as "unsold and destroyed" to the publisher, and neither the author nor the publisher has received any payment for this "stripped book".

No part of this publication may be reproduced in whole or in part, or stored in a retrieval system, or transmitted in any form or by any means, electronic, mechanical, photocopying, recording, or otherwise, without written permission of the publisher. For information regarding permission, write to Scholastic Inc. Attention: Permissions Department, 557 Broadway, New York, NY 10012.

ISBN 0-439-20420-8

Copyright © 2000 by Joanna Cole and Bruce Degen. All rights reserved. Published by Scholastic Inc. SCHOLASTIC, THE MAGIC SCHOOL BUS, and associated logos are trademarks and/or registered trademarks of Scholastic Inc.

69 68 67 66 65   20 21/0

Designed by Peter Koblish

Printed in the U.S.A.   40

INTRODUCTION

My name is Keesha. I am one of the kids in Ms. Frizzle's class.

Maybe you have heard of Ms. Frizzle. (Sometimes we just call her the Friz.) She is a terrific teacher — but a little strange. One of her favorite subjects is science, and she knows *everything* about it.

She takes us on lots of field trips in the Magic School Bus. Believe me, it's not called *magic* for nothing! We never know what's going to happen when we get on that bus.

Ms. Frizzle likes to surprise us, but we can usually tell when she is planning a special lesson — we just look at what she's wearing.

Not long ago, Ms. Frizzle showed up wearing this outfit. I didn't have a clue what kinds of weird creatures were on her dress. But I had a funny feeling we were going to find out. Was I ever right! Let me tell you what happened.

CHAPTER 1

"All right!" Ralphie waved his lunch bag and ran outside to the playground.

"This is great," said Wanda. "A picnic!"

None of us had been expecting Ms. Frizzle to take us outside for lunch. One minute, we were in our classroom ready to start our new science unit. The next, the Friz was taking us out to the picnic yard.

It just goes to show you: With Ms. Frizzle around, you should always expect the unexpected.

I wasn't going to complain. I love picnics! And the weather was perfect — warm and sunny with a clear blue sky.

1

"I feel lucky today," I said.

"The only kind of luck I ever have is *bad* luck," Arnold complained.

"Not *always*," insisted Dorothy Ann. (We usually just call her D.A.) She smiled into the sunshine as she sat down and began peeling her orange. "You're in Ms. Frizzle's class, aren't you?"

Arnold threw up his hands. "I rest my case!"

"I've got tuna fish. What about you, Keesha?" Tim asked.

It's a miracle of microbes!

I just wanted peanut butter and honey.

I didn't even have to look in my lunch bag. I already knew exactly what was inside. "Peanut butter and honey on my mom's homemade bread," I said. "My favorite!"

My mouth started watering. But when I took the sandwich from its wrapper, I saw some fuzzy blue-green spots on the bread.

"Eeewww! What is *that*?" I said.

Suddenly, I didn't feel so lucky anymore. Just looking at those spots made my stomach churn. But Ms. Frizzle's face lit up like a Christmas tree.

"That, Keesha, is one of the many miracles of microbes!" she announced.

"Huh? It just looks like mold to me," said Carlos.

"There's more to mold than meets the eye, Carlos. Lots more!" Ms. Frizzle said. "Each one of those spots of mold is actually made up of *millions* of tiny microbes."

"Microbes? What are they?" Tim asked.

D.A. flipped open her library book on microbes. She'd brought it outside with her lunch. "I think I can answer that. According to this, microbes are teeny tiny living creatures. They're too small to be seen without a microscope," she said. "Millions of microbes have to band together in order to be visible to the naked eye."

"Quite right. There's power in numbers, Dorothy Ann," said the Friz. "And microbes certainly have the numbers on their side. There are more microbes than any other living creature on Earth, and they are *everywhere*!"

4

From the Desk of Ms. Frizzle

Microbes Pass the Test of Time

Microbes have been on Earth for at least 3.5 *billion* years. That's longer than plants, dinosaurs, or any other living thing on the planet. And it's a *lot* longer than people have been around. Human beings didn't appear until just two million years ago.

Because microbes were the first life-forms on our planet, they are at the bottom of the food chain that feeds *all* life on Earth.

"At this very moment, microbes are floating in the air around us," Ms. Frizzle went on. "They are on our skin and teeth, inside our bodies, in the soil, in the food we eat, and on everything we touch. Every time you put a foot on the ground, you're stepping on *billions* of microbes."

Arnold looked around nervously. "I am? I think I'm going to be sick!"

"Some microbes *can* make us sick," Ms. Frizzle admitted. "Like viruses that cause chicken pox, and bacteria that cause strep throat."

Germs Make Me Sick
                    by Wanda

Microbes that can make you sick are called germs.

"Or when bacteria breaks through tooth enamel and causes tooth decay," D.A. added.

Ralphie ran his tongue across his teeth. "So *that's* how I got my cavity," he said.

This was more than I wanted to know. I just wanted to eat my lunch, but it was moldy with microbes!

"What about my sandwich?" I asked.

All of a sudden, Ms. Frizzle got a special twinkle in her eye — the same one we see whenever she's thinking of a far-out field trip.

"Excellent question, Keesha!" she said. "Class, it's time we got up close and personal with microbes. To the bus!"

Ms. Frizzle jumped to her feet and headed for the Magic School Bus. The next thing we knew, we were all inside the bus with her. I must have dropped my sandwich in the rush. When I looked out the window, I saw it lying on the ground next to the picnic table.

"Buckle up, everyone," said Ms. Frizzle. She got behind the wheel and pushed some buttons on the dashboard.

The bus got smaller and smaller. So did we! Soon we were no larger than a particle of dust.

"I guess you have to be microscopic if you want to mix with microbes," said Tim.

Now That's Small!
                    by Phoebe

We say that something is microscopic when it is too small to be seen without the use of a microscope.

"You said it!" Ms. Frizzle hit the gas pedal, and the bus shot up into the air. "Next stop, Keesha's sandwich!"

CHAPTER 2

The Magic School Bus flew through the air. Now that we were so tiny, we could see all kinds of creatures floating around us. Some looked like round balls. Others were shaped like rods or spirals.

"Are those microbes?" Arnold asked. He looked as if he was afraid to breathe. "Will they make us sick?"

"Not all microbes make us sick," said the Friz. "The few that do have given *all* microbes a bad name. Most people don't know that microbes do a lot more good than harm."

"You mean, a good microbe *isn't* hard to find?" Carlos said.

"Not at all!" the Friz answered.

Microbes Help Out!
by Wanda

Microbes may be small, but they help in big ways. The yeast that make bread rise are microbes. A lot of the oxygen we breathe is produced by microscopic algae. Fungi are used to make cheese (they put the *blue* in blue cheese), and different kinds of bacteria are used to make yogurt. Microbes are used to make medicines that keep us healthy, and they even clean nuclear waste. So hooray for microbes!

"Microbes come in all different sizes, shapes, and colors," Ms. Frizzle told us. She pulled out a poster from the glove compartment and unrolled it. It listed the five most common types of microbes.

MICROBES

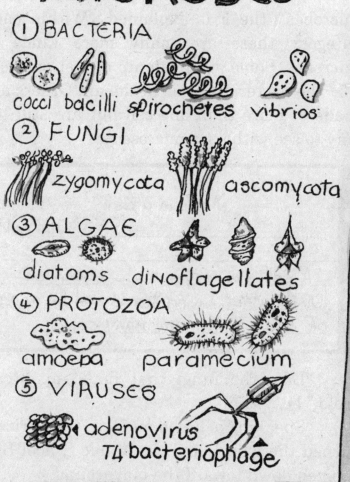

① BACTERIA

cocci bacilli spirochetes vibrios

② FUNGI

zygomycota   ascomycota

③ ALGAE

diatoms   dinoflagellates

④ PROTOZOA

amoeba   paramecium

⑤ VIRUSES

adenovirus
T4 bacteriophage

11

I couldn't believe all the funny-looking shapes!

"These are just a few examples of microbes," the Friz explained. "Within each category there are many more kinds of microbes. Some are made up of just one cell, like the bacteria we see in the air. Others are made of more than one cell but are still too tiny to see without a microscope."

What's in a Cell?

by Arnold

A cell is a very small, basic unit of living matter. Living things can be made of one cell or many, many cells.

"Like the fungi that make up bread mold," D.A. said.

"Speaking of bread mold . . ." Ms. Frizzle turned the wheel, and the Magic School Bus zoomed down toward the playground.

I saw my sandwich on the ground next

to the picnic table. The closer we flew, the bigger it looked! The mold was like a huge forest next to a sandy beach of bread. Ms. Frizzle aimed the bus at one of the spots of mold, and we plunged right in.

Yuck! I definitely wasn't hungry anymore.

After we landed, Ms. Frizzle handed out rubber boots and safety helmets. Then we all jumped off the Magic School Bus, right onto the surface of the bread. It was spongy — and tricky to walk on. The air holes in my bread were like big craters.

"Wow!" D.A. said. "This is mold?"

It looked more like a forest to me. We were surrounded by tall, smooth treelike stalks. Each stalk blossomed into a cluster of smaller branches at the top. There were so many, I couldn't begin to count them all.

"Yes indeed. Fabulous fungi as far as the eye can see," Ms. Frizzle announced, looking at the fungi with a smile.

"But . . . what are the fungi doing here?" Phoebe asked.

Can You See the Fungus Among Us?
(If you can, it isn't a microbe!)
by Carlos

Most fungi are microscopic. But some are larger, like mushrooms we find in forests and lichens that grow on trees and fallen logs. Once a single fungus is big enough to see with the naked eye, it isn't called a microbe anymore.

One type of fungus, called *Armillaria bulbosa*, grows to be very big. There's a single *Armillaria bulbosa* in Michigan that weighs more than ten tons and stretches across almost forty acres of land! It's so big that it has a nickname – the Humongous Fungus.

"They're doing what microbes do best, Phoebe," Ms. Frizzle said. "Eating and reproducing."

"You mean, these fungi are chowing down on Keesha's bread?" asked Ralphie.

Ms. Frizzle gave a contented nod. "Isn't it amazing? Most microbes such as fungi and bacteria can't make their own food. They get their food from other animals or plants — like the wheat in Keesha's bread. And when they eat, big changes take place."

"You mean, *sloppy* changes," I said. My boots had started sinking into the soggy part of my sandwich. "My bread is rotting!"

Eating With Enzymes
by Ralphie

Fungi and bacteria produce substances called enzymes that help them eat. Enzymes break down food into simpler materials the microbes can absorb.

"So, these fungi are changing Keesha's bread by making it rot so they can use it for food!" Tim said.

"Precisely!" the Friz told him.

I was still trying to keep my balance on that slippery stuff. But I got the picture. Rotting food was good for microbes.

And bad, *bad* luck for me!

"How did so many fungi get here so fast?" I asked. "My mom just made this bread last weekend. I didn't see a bit of mold until today."

"Look up," the Friz instructed.

When we did, we saw dozens of bluish-green balls attached to the top of each fungus.

"Those are spores," Ms. Frizzle explained.

The Scoop on Spores
by Keesha

Ever wonder what makes bread mold so fuzzy and colorful? Spores do! Bread molds can be black, blue-green, or pink, depending on the color of the spores.

"Spores are like seeds. They're carried to new places by the wind or by animals, and new fungi grow from them," the Friz explained.

"So with the help of spores, each fungus produces dozens of new fungi," Wanda said. "These microbes sure know how to get around."

"They work fast, too," D.A. said, looking at her book. "Some microbes can double their numbers in less than ten minutes."

"No *wonder* there's a lot more than just one fungus among us," Carlos joked.

More, More, More Microbes!
by Tim

Different microbes have different ways of reproducing. Fungi make spores. Yeast cells form buds that develop into new yeast cells. And bacteria simply split in two.

I did some math in my head. "Wait a minute. If microbes reproduce that fast, wouldn't they totally overrun *everything*?" I asked.

"They would — *if* conditions for growth were perfect," said Ms. Frizzle. "But if their food runs out, or if it gets too crowded, or too hot, or too cold, then microbes start to die out."

Phoebe took a look in D.A.'s book. "According to this, lots of packaged foods like hot dogs and rolls contain preservatives that slow down the growth of microbes and keep food from spoiling," she said. "But homemade foods, like your mom's bread, don't have preservatives."

Where Do Microbes Live?
by Arnold

Most microbes grow best where it's moist and dark. They don't like it too hot or too cold. That's why we refrigerate some foods.

The cold air inside the refrigerator slows down microbes.
 But microbes do like it sweet!
Sugar helps microbes to reproduce faster. Substances with acid in them – like lemon juice, and vinegar used for pickling vegetables – make it harder for microbes to grow.

"So *that's* why it's a moldy mess!" I said.

All of a sudden, everything started shaking. "Whoa!" I grabbed at the tubular stalks of fungi to keep from falling.

"Earthquake!" Arnold cried.

"Relax. It's just the fourth-grade kids cleaning up," said Tim.

The fourth graders in our school had started a compost heap and recycling program. They towered over us as they collected trash and food scraps from the playground. We were so tiny that they looked like skyscrapers! No, bigger — like huge mountains! Every time one of the kids took a step, the ground trembled like crazy.

"I never knew exploring microbes would be such a *shaky* experience," Ralphie said.

"Don't look now, but this could become a *squishy* experience soon," said Phoebe.

Phoebe pointed toward a fourth-grade girl who was walking toward us. The girl wore gloves and was busy dropping D.A.'s orange peel into her bag of food scraps. She didn't seem to notice my sandwich lying on the ground in front of her — with all of us on it.

We could see her enormous foot coming toward us. "Our luck is running out, guys," I cried. "The Magic School Bus is about to turn into the Magic Pancake!"

CHAPTER 3

"I *told* you I always have bad luck!" Arnold groaned.

"And now it's rubbing off on us!" said Ralphie.

"To the bus, everyone!" Ms. Frizzle instructed.

We didn't have to be told twice. We all ran for the Magic School Bus — pronto!

As I scrambled in, a dark shadow fell over us. I looked out the window and saw the gigantic sole of the girl's sneaker right above the bus.

"No!" I cried.

I waited for the sneaker to come crashing

down on us. But at the last second, the girl paused.

"What's *this* doing on the ground?" she murmured.

Everyone cheered as the fourth grader picked up my sandwich and tossed it into her bag.

"I guess your luck is changing for the better, Arnold," I said.

Boy, was I wrong! A few moments later, we all bounced around inside the Magic School Bus as the giant fourth grader emptied the scrap food from her bag into the compost bin.

"Yuck!" said Phoebe. She pointed at the bits of bread, orange peel, and dead leaves that were crammed against the windows of the bus. "We were never thrown in with the trash at my old school."

"This might look like trash to you," said the Friz. "But to microbes, it's a feast!"

"You mean microbes are eating the food in this compost bin, the same way they were eating my bread?" I asked.

23

The Dirt on Compost
by Carlos

Compost is a mixture of leaves, vegetables, and other matter that is in the process of decaying. Once the material is completely decomposed, it becomes the soft, dark, nonrocky part of the soil, which is called humus. Humus is full of rich nutrients for growing plants.

← food scraps and plants

partially decomposed compost

mostly decomposed compost

humus

Compost heap

"That's right. Take a look." Ms. Frizzle touched a button on the dashboard, and the bus got a little bigger. We were still pretty small. But now we could see a little farther, over the tops of fungi like the ones on my bread.

24

"It's microbe mania out there!" Arnold said.

He wasn't kidding, either. All around us were colonies of fungi — and plenty of other microbes, too. We saw some of the same kinds of creatures we'd seen floating in the air — balls, rods, and spirals. Only here, millions of each kind were all piled together.

"Those are bacteria," Ms. Frizzle told us. "Just like fungi, they need to be around plant or animal matter that they can use for food. Hundreds of different kinds of microbes are at work here, producing enzymes that break down the old food and plants into food the microbes can absorb."

"That means microbes are making big changes to their environment," D.A. added. "After the enzymes do their work, all this stuff turns into humus and carbon dioxide gas."

Ms. Frizzle steered the Magic School Bus across the food, leaves, and branches in the compost bin. It was like a gigantic jungle! Microbes were plastered all over everything. Fungi and bacteria were producing enzymes that made old food and leaves and branches decay. As everything rotted, we could see carbon dioxide gas bubble up into the air.

Decomposition Is a Gas!
by Keesha

When microbes break down food scraps, plants, and animals, it's called decomposition. When materials decompose, the process produces carbon dioxide gas that becomes part of the air we breathe. (Carbon dioxide is what makes the bubbles in carbonated drinks and the holes in bread.)

The stuff that's left over — humus — doesn't take up nearly as much space as the food scraps did before they were broken down. So a lot of compost makes a little soil.

But that wasn't all. We could also see waves of heat rising off the compost.

"Why is it so *hot* here?" Ralphie asked, wiping his brow. "I'm sweating!"

"It takes a lot of energy to turn all this scrap food and grass and leaves into fresh earth and carbon dioxide gas," Ms. Frizzle explained. "These microbes are working so hard they actually make the compost heat up."

Ms. Frizzle turned the wheel, and the bus began to burrow *into* the food and leaves. Near the top, the food scraps and plants hadn't changed very much. But farther down, it all just looked like brown mush.

"*Yee-ha!*" the Friz cried as the bus slid around on the stuff.

"You call this fun?" Phoebe asked. She was clutching the seat in front of her.

"According to my research, microbes have been at work longer down here," D.A. said. "The food and branches and stuff have already totally broken down to fresh humus."

"So, when microbes break down food like my bread, it *is* a good thing," I said.

"Microbes are the best waste management program on the planet," said Ms. Frizzle. "Without them, old food and plants and animals would all just pile up. But with microbes they break down to humus."

"It's a *rotten* job," said Carlos. "Luckily, microbes are very good at it."

We all groaned. "Carlos!"

"Microbes are always changing their environment because that's how they get the food they need to grow and make more of themselves," Ms. Frizzle went on. "Sure, a few microbes do damage when they grow inside people or on plants. But many, many *more* microbes do good!"

From the Desk of Ms. Frizzle

Microbe Against Microbe

Some microbes actually eat other kinds of microbes that can make plants or animals sick. Lifesaving medicines called **antibiotics** are made from bacteria and fungi. Those antibiotics kill disease-causing bacteria, so people can get well.

"According to my book, some bacteria actually clean up toxic waste," D.A. said. "They use poisons like oil, pesticides, and methane gas for food, and break them down into simpler materials that *don't* hurt the environment."

"Wow," I said. Hearing so many good things about microbes was making me feel *lucky* to have those microscopic creatures around!

"What about that microbe over there?" Carlos asked. "What's *it* doing?"

He pointed to a long hairy-looking creature that was headed our way.

"That is a kind of protozoa," Ms. Frizzle said. "A protozoan is different from the other microbes we've seen. Unlike fungi and bacteria, a protozoan can swallow its food without breaking it down into simpler materials first."

"Um . . . does anyone else have the feeling that protozoan thinks we're a snack?" Arnold asked.

The protozoan looked like it was crawling on its tiny hairs as it came closer to the Magic School Bus.

Fortunately, we were quicker than it was. Ms. Frizzle hit the gas, and we were out of there in a flash.

"Faster than a speeding microbe," Carlos said as the bus zoomed upward. We were back at the top of the compost bin in no time.

"Phew!" I said. "Luck was on our side this time."

I should have known it was too good to last.

A loud buzzing sound made me look up. "Uh-oh," I said. "Flies!"

Dozens of flies swarmed overhead. We were so small that their bulging eyes seemed enormous! Their hairy black legs had microbes stuck all over them. Every time one of those flies buzzed toward us, my stomach did a flip.

All of a sudden, a fly landed with its leg on top of the Magic School Bus and began to eat from the compost.

"I guess microbes aren't the only creatures that like to chow down on leftovers," Tim said.

"Gross," said Arnold.

But that wasn't nearly as gross as what happened when the fly flew off.

"We're stuck to the fly's foot!" Phoebe cried.

As the fly buzzed up into the air, the Magic School Bus — with all of us inside — went with it.

CHAPTER 4

The Magic School Bus swayed from side to side, dangling from the fly's foot.

"Yuck!" I said. "Hanging around with flies is *not* my idea of fun."

"Microbes do it all the time," Ms. Frizzle told us.

She pointed to the microbes that covered the fly's sticky legs. "Flies are like passenger jets for microbes. They're a great way for microbes to travel," she said.

"I wish we knew where we are going," D.A. said. "What if this fly is heading to the Dumpster behind the cafeteria for some dessert?"

Flies Spread Disease

by Tim

Flies pick up lots of microbes during their travels, including microbes that can make us sick. They are one way diseases are carried from place to place, and from person to person.

Luckily, the fly buzzed around to the front of the school instead. It flew right through the open door of a minivan parked at the curb.

Jimmy, one of the fourth-grade boys, was just climbing into the van. The fly landed on him. When it took off again, the Magic School Bus was stuck on Jimmy's shirt.

"What a break!" Wanda heaved a sigh of relief. "No more flights on a fly's foot for me, thanks," she said.

I felt lucky, too — until I took a closer look at Jimmy.

"Thanks for picking me up, Mom. My throat really hurts," Jimmy said, coughing. His nose was red and swollen, and his eyes were watery.

Jimmy's mother turned around from the front seat and handed him a tissue. "I'm taking you straight home to bed," she said.

"Uh-oh. Jimmy's *sick*," Arnold moaned. "And we're stuck to his shirt!"

"*Ahh . . . ahhh . . . choo!*"

Jimmy let out a deafening sneeze.

All of a sudden, we were bombarded by a huge cloud of the smallest creatures I had ever seen. They were a lot smaller than the other microbes we had met. They looked like teeny, tiny Ping-Pong balls with spikes all around them. Billions of them came shooting out of Jimmy's mouth — straight at the Magic School Bus.

"There's good news, and there's bad news, class," Ms. Frizzle announced. "The good news is that we are now getting a fabulous firsthand look at another kind of microbe. Viruses!"

"If that's the good news," Tim said, "I really don't want to hear the bad news."

"The bad news is that those viruses cause the common cold," the Friz explained. "If we're not careful, we'll get sick, too."

CHAPTER 5

How much more bad luck could we have? We really deserved a break. But did we get one? No way!

Viruses kept shooting toward us. I was really glad all the windows on the Magic School Bus were shut tight! The viruses all bounced off without getting inside.

"Those viruses look much smaller than the other microbes we've seen," Tim pointed out. "Are *all* viruses that tiny?"

"Some are even tinier," D.A. said. "According to my book, viruses can be twenty to a hundred times smaller than bacteria."

Carlos watched as some of the viruses landed on Jimmy's shirt near the Magic School Bus. "So, can viruses be helpful, like bacteria and fungi?" he asked. "Do any of them clean up toxic waste, or help plants and animals to break down into fresh earth?"

Wanda borrowed D.A.'s book and took a look. "All viruses have just one purpose," she said. "To make more of themselves. And to do that, they have to invade living cells."

A Variety of Viruses
                    by Wanda

Did you know there are more than two hundred different viruses that can cause you to get a cold? No wonder colds are so common — and so hard to cure!

"Just keep them away from me," Arnold said.

"Our tiny viral friends are very unusual," Ms. Frizzle said. "They are really only half-alive. Viruses show no sign of life at all when they are on their own. But once they come in contact with something that's alive, they invade it. Then they become very active and do what microbes do best."

"Reproduce!" we all shouted.

"I guess microbes just can't get enough of themselves," Carlos joked.

"The trouble is, viruses damage the cells they invade," the Friz told us. "And when that happens, the plant or animal or person being infected can get sick."

"So," I said, "when you talk about the few microbes that can hurt us, viruses go on the list."

"You hit it on the nose, Keesha!" Ms. Frizzle exclaimed.

At that moment, Jimmy sneezed. Then he reached over and closed the minivan door. His mom started the engine, and we were off.

"Great. We're on the road with a walking germ factory," Arnold said.

"Not to worry, Arnold! The good news is that our bodies come equipped with lots of natural defenses to keep viruses and other microbes from making us sick," Ms. Frizzle said.

From D.A.'s Notebook

Our skin is like natural armor. It keeps microbes from getting into our bodies. So do our eyelashes and nasal hairs, and even the tears in our eyes.

We have defenses inside our bodies, too. Saliva and mucus make surfaces slippery, so it's hard for microbes to get into our cells and do damage.

YOUR NATURAL ARMOR

SKIN

EYE LASHES

TEARS

NASAL HAIRS

We were sure glad to hear that. None of us wanted to catch Jimmy's cold.

"What made Jimmy's germ defense system break down?" Ralphie asked.

"Sometimes, microbes manage to get into our bodies despite our natural defenses," Ms. Frizzle explained. "When a lot of microbes get in all at once, or when they grow very fast, then we get sick."

How Germs Invade
by Carlos

Germs can get into our bodies through open cuts, or from germy hands being put in our mouths. Some germs simply fight their way past our nasal hairs and eyelashes.

> When we are run-down due to lack of sleep or not eating well, microbes are more likely to get into our bodies. We have a hard time resisting new germs, too — ones our bodies aren't used to.

"My mom makes a big deal about how important it is to keep clean," Phoebe said. "Does that really help us to stay healthy?"

"Absolutely, Phoebe!" the Friz said. "By washing our skin — especially our hands — and clothes, we keep away microbes that could make us sick."

We were all glad to see that Jimmy's mom made Jimmy change into clean pajamas after they got home.

"Excellent," Ms. Frizzle said. "Now the viruses on Jimmy's shirt won't be able to get back inside his body to do more harm. They'll all come out in the wash."

"What about us?" I wondered. "*We're* still stuck to Jimmy's shirt."

Just then, Jimmy's mother tossed Jimmy's dirty shirt into the washing machine in the kitchen — and we went with it. Oh, bad! Oh, bad! Oh, bad!

"I hope no one gets seasick," Carlos said. "We're in for a wet and wild ride!"

CHAPTER 6

Being in that washer was like having a huge waterfall crash down on us. I was starting to feel as if this were the *un*luckiest day of my life.

"Time for the shield," Ms. Frizzle said.

She hit a button on the dashboard and a thick, clear shield went up around the bus. "There! That will keep the water and heat *outside* the bus where they can't hurt us."

And not a moment too soon. Hot, soapy water was already gushing all around us like a gigantic car wash.

"Look! The viruses are getting washed away," Wanda said.

The soapy water made everything outside the bus slippery. As we watched, the tiny cold-causing viruses slid away from Jimmy's shirt and swirled harmlessly in the water.

"Soap makes everything so slick that it's difficult for viruses and other microbes to stick to anything," Ms. Frizzle said. "And if they can't stick, they can't make you sick."

Arnold's How-to Hand-Washing Guide

1. Use plenty of soap and warm water.
2. Wash the palms, fingers, wrists, and the back of the hands. Don't forget to scrub under the fingernails!
3. Wash for at least 10-15 seconds. That's enough time to wash away most microbes.
4. Rinse!
5. Dry your hands on your own towel or on a clean paper towel.

"Keeping clean is the way to stay microbe-free," Carlos said.

Just then, the soapy water made the Magic School Bus slide away from Jimmy's shirt. We swished and swirled about. With all the bad luck we'd had so far, I was sure we were going to get washed down the drain with the water and cold-causing viruses.

But guess what? When the wash and rinse cycles were all finished, we wound up perched on one of the wet folds of Jimmy's shirt.

"At least it's clean," Phoebe said. "No microbes!"

From the Desk of Ms. Frizzle

Don't Forget to Wash Your Hands!

If you touch your own eyes, mouth, nose, or open cuts with germy hands, germs can get inside your body and make you sick.

Touching other people with germy hands can make *them* sick. That's why you should wash microbes away with soapy water.

Be sure to wash *before* you:
• prepare or eat food
• treat a cut or take care of someone who is sick

Be sure to wash *after* you:
• go to the bathroom
• handle raw meat
• blow your nose, cough, or sneeze
• handle garbage
• are around someone who is sick
• play with or touch a pet

We all felt a jolt as Jimmy's mom pulled the shirt from the washing machine. We could see her give it a stiff shake, and then the Magic School Bus went flying across the kitchen.

Plop! The next thing we knew, we had landed in a mound of sticky, moist dough. My mom does a lot of baking, so I knew exactly what the sticky stuff was.

"We're on top of some homemade bread dough," I told everyone.

Jimmy's father began to pat the dough down into a loaf pan.

There was just one problem. The Magic School Bus was being patted, too! Right down inside the dough.

"This is what I call a *sticky* situation," Carlos said.

The dough was already starting to cover the windows of the bus. The last thing I saw was the smiling face of Jimmy's father as he slid the loaf pan full of dough — and us — inside the oven to bake.

"What's he so happy about?" I said. "We're about to be baked to a crisp!"

CHAPTER 7

"Just our luck," said Tim. "We start out having a picnic lunch, and we wind up getting cooked!"

"We'll be fine. The heat shield is still on," the Friz said. I was still a little worried.

"Isn't it marvelous?" the Friz said. "Microbes are hard at work here, too. Look at those yeast cells!"

Outside the bus windows, I saw balloon-shaped cells mixed in with the dough. There were pockets of air around some of them.

"Yeast is a kind of fungus," Wanda said, looking in D.A.'s book. "According to this, it makes bread rise."

"Right you are, Wanda!" said Ms. Frizzle. "Yeast cells produce enzymes that break down the natural sugars in the bread dough into simpler materials the yeast cells can use for food. That's how yeast gets the energy it needs to make more yeast cells."

What Is Fermentation?
by Tim

When microbes use enzymes to break down sugars into simpler materials, we call the process fermentation.

"Just like the microbes in the compost bin make enzymes that break down old plants and animals into food *they* can use," Wanda said.

"Precisely!" Ms. Frizzle told her.

"Does that mean these yeast cells will make fresh soil and carbon dioxide gas, like the microbes in the compost bin?" Tim asked.

Arnold wrinkled up his nose. "I don't think I want dirt in my bread."

"Actually, different microbes produce different by-products," Ms. Frizzle said. "This yeast won't make fresh earth, but it will make plenty of carbon dioxide gas. That's what makes the bread spongy and light."

We could see exactly what the Friz was talking about. All around us, gas bubbled up around the yeast cells. The bread got puffier and puffier.

"So, yeast goes on our most-wanted list of microbes," Carlos said. "We *want* it to make bread rise!"

What Good Are Enzymes?
by Ralphie

Microbial enzymes are good for a lot more than just making bread rise. They are also used to make cheese, yogurt, soy sauce, paper, laundry detergent, bubble gum, and the stonewashed look on blue jeans.

"I'm starting to get the picture," Arnold said. "Microbes really do a lot of good."

"*I'm* starting to get hungry," Ralphie said.

He wasn't the only one. We had all left our lunches in the playground at school. By the time the bread finished baking and Jimmy's dad took it out of the oven, our stomachs were growling like crazy!

We couldn't see beyond the bread that surrounded us. But *something* was going on. I could feel the loaf shaking.

"What's happening now?" I asked.

A second later, I found out. The razor-sharp blade of a knife sliced through the bread right next to the Magic School Bus. Did I ever jump!

The next thing we knew, we were sitting on top of a freshly cut slice that Jimmy's dad placed on a plate. He carried it into the family room, where Jimmy was resting on the couch with a blanket over him.

"This will help you feel better," his dad announced.

"Mmmm." Jimmy picked up the slice of warm bread.

Being Healthy Helps You
Stay Germ-Free
by Keesha

Eating good foods — like whole grains and fresh fruits and vegetables — helps you to stay healthy. The right foods give your body the energy it needs to fight off disease-causing microbes.

Phoebe started to look worried. "If Jimmy sneezed out all those cold viruses, there are probably more *inside* his body, right?" she asked.

"*Lots* more!" Ms. Frizzle told her. "They're inside Jimmy's nose and throat, battling against the natural defense systems in his body."

The Friz grinned as Jimmy popped the bread into his mouth. "Get ready for more action and adventure," she said. "We're going down the hatch!"

CHAPTER 8

What?! I couldn't believe we were actually heading into Jimmy's body. How much worse could our luck get!?

We were about to find out.

The Magic School Bus slid to the back of Jimmy's throat along with his bread. His throat looked really red and swollen. But that wasn't the only thing we noticed.

"Yikes! Look at all those viruses," D.A. said.

Tiny cold-causing viruses were stuck all over the cells lining Jimmy's throat.

"Those viruses are invading Jimmy's

cells and making him sick," Ms. Frizzle explained.

"But . . . how?" I wondered.

Ms. Frizzle tapped some buttons on the dashboard. The next thing we knew, the Magic School Bus shrank right down to virus size.

"Let's hitch a ride with that virus and see how it's done," said the Friz.

She steered the bus over to one of the spiky, round viruses. "This virus may seem small. But it's capable of doing *big* damage," she said.

As we watched, the virus used its spikes to drill into one of the cells lining Jimmy's throat.

"Those viruses weren't moving at all when we saw them outside Jimmy's body," Tim said. "But now they're really coming alive!"

The spiked virus dug deeper and deeper, until it was actually *inside* Jimmy's cell. And then the Magic School Bus slipped in behind it!

I could think of a million places I'd rather be — like having lunch in a nice, clean, *germ-free* restaurant. But no such luck.

"Viruses lead exciting lives when they're around living cells," Ms. Frizzle told us. "This virus is using the material inside Jimmy's cell to make more viruses. And we're right here to see it happen. What luck!"

Arnold's face was white. "*Bad* luck, you mean," he said. "Very bad."

I had to admit the situation was serious. Jimmy's cell was already filling up with other, spiked viruses. They grew thicker and thicker around us.

"We need some crowd control in here," Phoebe said.

But those viruses were completely *out* of control. Before long, there were so many new viruses that Jimmy's cell actually burst open.

"The viruses *killed* Jimmy's cell," Carlos said.

"And look! All the new viruses are attacking *more* of Jimmy's cells. No wonder he's sick," I said.

I couldn't believe it. The viruses were everywhere!

"The giant germ is certainly hard at work," Ms. Frizzle said.

Ralphie stared out a bus window. "But those viruses are tiny!"

"Microbes may be small," said the Friz. "But there are a lot of them, and the changes they make can be *giant,* whether they turn old food and leaves into humus, or —"

"Make a mess out of Jimmy's throat!" Arnold finished.

A Few Good Microbes
by Keesha

Remember that microbes are not all bad. Some microbes provide our bodies with protein or important vitamins. Others crowd out harmful bacteria, or make acids that keep harmful bacteria from multiplying and making us sick.

"Not to worry, class. Jimmy's body is already hard at work fighting the viruses," Ms. Frizzle assured us.

Ms. Frizzle turned the wheel and drove the Magic School Bus straight through Jimmy's throat cells. Soon we found ourselves inside one of the blood vessels that carried blood through Jimmy's body.

"Whoa!" I grabbed my seat as the Magic School Bus was swept up by the fluid. "Talk about speedy. This blood is moving fast!"

Arnold groaned, covering his eyes. "Tell me when it's over."

The Magic School Bus rushed along the blood vessel. The liquid part of the blood was clear. But there were lots of cells racing through the blood vessel with us.

Ms. Frizzle pointed to some red, saucer-shaped cells outside the bus windows. "Those are red blood cells. They make our blood look red," she said. "Their job is to bring oxygen to all the different parts of the body."

"What about those white blobs?" Phoebe asked. She pointed to some white cells that rushed alongside us in the clear liquid of the blood.

"Ah, wonderful white blood cells! Our body's biggest defense against microbes that make us sick," said the Friz. "They travel through the blood in our body, gobbling up germs wherever they find them."

"So, Jimmy's white blood cells are like an army that's fighting against the viruses in his body," Tim said.

"Correct you are, Tim," the Friz said.

From the Desk of Ms. Frizzle

Some Sore Throats Are Caused by Bacteria

Viruses aren't the only microbes that can give us a sore throat. Sore throats can be caused by bacteria, too.

Bacteria such as **streptococci,** which cause strep throat, attack the cells in our throat. Long strings of bacteria work together and reproduce by dividing in two. If the bacteria reproduce faster than white blood cells can destroy them, our throat becomes infected and we get sick.

We all watched as the white blood cells attacked the viruses in Jimmy's throat. The white blobs reached out and engulfed virus after virus. The white blood cells actually *ate* the viruses.

"But there are so *many* viruses. Can the white blood cells really kill them all?" Ralphie asked.

"Our bodies have ways of helping white blood cells to work better and faster," Ms. Frizzle told him. "When there's an infection, we pump extra blood to the spot. That way there are more white blood cells to destroy the microbes."

"So *that's* why we're moving so fast," I said.

The Friz nodded. "All that extra blood is what makes Jimmy's throat and nose red and swollen, too. Even feeling tired and achy is a good sign. Jimmy feels that way because his body is using so much energy to destroy the viruses."

Fevers Are Germ Fighters
by Ralphie

When we're sick, our body temperature goes up. That's because white blood cells reproduce faster and work better against viruses at a hotter temperature.

"So, lots of the things that make Jimmy feel sick are actually signs that his body is doing a good job fighting the germs!" Arnold said.

"The workings of the human body are a wonder to behold," said the Friz. "Within a few days, Jimmy's natural defenses will defeat the viruses, and he'll be well again."

I was really glad to hear that. If only *our* luck would change for the better, too!

Q. Can Antibiotics Kill Viruses?
A. No Way!
by Wanda

Antibiotics are medicines made from microbes. Antibiotics kill bacteria. They do a great job of curing diseases caused by bacteria, like pneumonia and strep throat. But antibiotics can't cure diseases caused by viruses, like measles, chicken pox, colds, and flus. It's up to white blood cells to win that battle.

Outside the bus, a white blood cell sprayed some viruses with a cloud of tiny white particles.

"Check it out. That white blood cell just sprayed antibodies," D.A. said, referring to her book. "That's how white blood cells mark invaders like viruses and bacteria so other white blood cells know what to destroy."

"Those antibodies have another job, too," said Ms. Frizzle. "They keep track of the disease-causing microbes they meet in the body so they can help fight them off faster the next time."

"So, next time those viruses try to invade, Jimmy's body will probably be able to fight them off before he even gets sick," I said. "Now *that's* good medicine."

"And Jimmy's body is doing it all on its own," Carlos said. "I never knew our bodies were so good at taking care of themselves."

From the Desk of Ms. Frizzle

Vaccines Work Against Viruses

A vaccine is a shot that helps your body to resist viruses. Here's how it works:

1. Weakened germs are injected into your body. These germs are harmless, but they are very similar to germs that can make you sick.

2. Your body's white blood cells go to work fighting the germs. Antibodies remember the germs, so your body is prepared to fight them even better in the future.

3. When the real, harmful germs come along, your body is able to kill them off before they can make you sick.

Unfortunately, there is no vaccine for the common cold.

Just then, a white blood cell sprayed a cloud of antibodies all over the bus.

"Uh-oh," Phoebe said. "Now Jimmy's white blood cells see *us* as an invader."

"They think we are a virus!" Ralphie yelled.

"Jimmy's natural defenses are working perfectly!" Ms. Frizzle announced.

The rest of us didn't feel quite so enthusiastic. Especially when we noticed a white blood cell coming up from behind.

I waited for a stroke of good luck. We really needed one. But that white blood cell kept stretching toward the Magic School Bus.

"If that white blood cell does its job," I said, "we're history."

CHAPTER 9

"No need to panic," said Ms. Frizzle. "The Magic School Bus has one thing white blood cells don't."

"What's that?" I asked.

"A turbo-charged engine!"

Ms. Frizzle hit the gas, and we zoomed away from the white blood cell.

"Hooray!" we cheered.

The Magic School Bus sped through Jimmy's cells until we found ourselves back inside the huge cavern of his mouth again.

There were a lot more white blood cells now. We saw plenty of viruses, too. But the

white blood cells were doing a great job of attacking them.

"Jimmy's going to be better in no time," Wanda said.

Just then, Jimmy's mouth opened, and daylight flooded over us.

"Ahh . . . ahhh . . ."

We knew what was coming next.

"Chooo!"

Jimmy sneezed. The tremendous force of it sent the Magic School Bus flying out of his mouth.

We spun wildly through the air. It was hard to tell exactly where we were. But when I saw a blur of green trees and blue sky, I knew we weren't indoors anymore.

"We shot right out the open window!" Ralphie said.

We landed on the street and — *pop!* — the Magic School Bus returned to its normal size.

"What a wild ride!" Tim said.

I heard a loud rumbling. But it wasn't coming from the engine. It was our stomachs growling! And the loudest stomach of all was our driver's — the Friz!

"Next stop, Paolo's Pizza!" Ms. Frizzle announced.

That was music to our ears. Paolo's makes the best pizza!

"I guess our luck is changing for the better after all," I said as we got off the bus in the parking lot.

"I always feel that way — *after* the Friz's field trips are over," Arnold said.

He pulled open the door to Paolo's, and we all went inside. We couldn't wait to eat!

But first we stopped to wash our hands with soap and water. We'd had enough microbes for one day.

FREE PUBLIC LIBRARY UNION, NEW JERSEY

3 9549 00563 8789